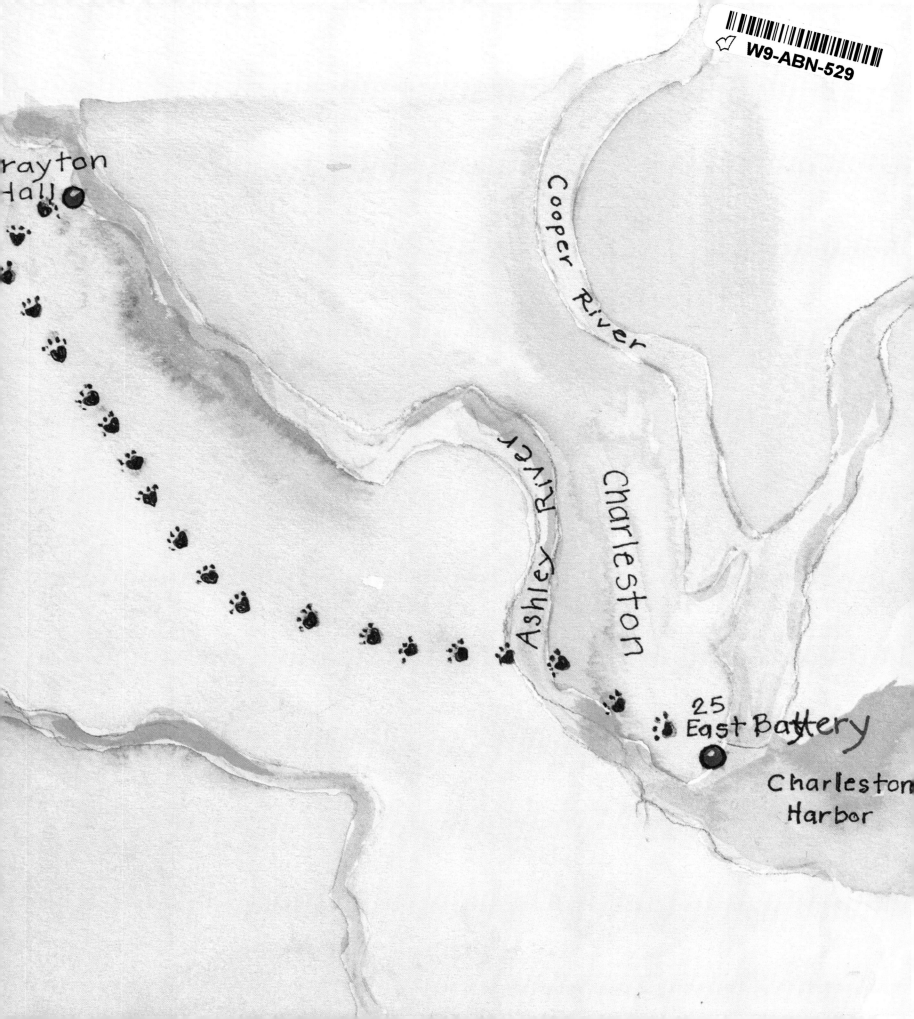

Nipper of Drayton Hall

Young
Palmetto
Books

Kim Shealy Jeffcoat, Series Editor

Nipper
of Drayton Hall

Amey Lewis

Illustrations by Gerry McElroy

Foreword by Stephanie Meeks

The University of South Carolina Press

© 2015 University of South Carolina

Published by the University of South Carolina Press
Columbia, South Carolina 29208

www.sc.edu/uscpress

Manufactured in the United States of America

24 23 22 21 20 19 18 17 16 15   10 9 8 7 6 5 4 3 2 1

Library of Congress Cataloging-in-Publication Data can
be found at http://catalog.loc.gov/.

ISBN: 978-1-61117-625-4 (hardcover)
ISBN: 978-1-61117-626-1 (paperback)
ISBN: 978-1-61117-627-8 (ebook)

The just-about-true story of a real dog named Nipper,
and of a real Charleston lady named Charlotta Drayton,
and of a real boy named Richmond Bowens,
and, finally, of the very real place they all loved:
Drayton Hall.

The story takes place one fine spring day in 1916.

Dedicated to my best friend,
Anne Drayton Nelson

Contents

Foreword

Historic preservation is not just about saving old places. Just as important, it is about preserving the stories of those places, and the people who loved and cared for them.

This book is just that! It is the story about real people and a real dog from an earlier time, all of whom loved Drayton Hall. Today, this amazing place—the oldest preserved plantation house in America that is open to the public—and the many places portrayed in this book are still there for you to discover. As you explore the rooms and grounds where Nipper once played, I hope you will remember his story and that of his dear friends, Charlotta Drayton and Richmond Bowens, and the wonderful day they spent here so many years ago.

Stephanie Meeks

President and CEO, National Trust for Historic Preservation

25 East Battery

Leaving Charleston

My name is Nipper. I am a dog . . . a good dog, but a dog nevertheless. I yip on a regular basis, and I nip, but only when I am happy. Oh, and also I growl, but only when I am scared. Charlotta Drayton and I live most of the year in our house at 25 East Battery in Charleston, South Carolina.

Every year early in April, about the time the azaleas are showing off and the magnolias are blooming, we leave our town house so we can spend six weeks in the country at Charlotta's family home, Drayton Hall. Sammy is waiting outside. He takes care of things for us all around the house and also drives Charlotta when she needs to go places. He has polished the car, so it is very shiny. I have had my bath, so I shine too. Emma, Sammy's wife, has packed the trunks and gathered the groceries. Charlotta has collected a few books and her painting supplies.

"Time to head to Drayton Hall," she says.

I give an excited yip, nip the air, and then grab my favorite red ball!

I hope Richmond Bowens will be there. He is my friend.

"Is everyone ready?" asks Sammy. "Come along, little Nipper."

The Arrival

A Long Ride

It is a very long ride from Charleston to Drayton Hall so I nap in the car, but when I hear Charlotta say, "Wake up, Nipper," I perk up my ears and open my eyes because I know we are near the brick entrance. I stand up tall and start to yip. I snatch my ball and wiggle until I can pop my head out of the window. Sammy shifts gears, and we lurch forward. We pass my friend Richmond Bowens' house on the way down the dirt road. Suddenly there it is–Drayton Hall–at the end of the long drive.

Wait . . . I think I spy my friend Richmond!

As soon as the car comes to a halt and Charlotta opens the door, I jump down and begin yipping and nipping into the air. I turn a few circles because Charlotta likes it when I show off a bit. She smiles at me and then says hello to Richmond.

"Welcome back, Miss Drayton. Hello, Little Business Man." Richmond laughs and says, "I call you Business Man, little puppy dog, because you just mind your own business while checkin' on everybody else's."

Charlotta, Emma, and Sammy laugh and clap their hands.

I just "Yip!"

We all love it here, but Charlotta loves it the most. Drayton Hall has been in her family since 1738. That's a long time, and it is one reason she gets a dreamy look on her face when she sees the house. Charlotta wishes Drayton Hall might stay the same forever and ever just the way it is today.

"Your family may have been here as long as the Draytons," Charlotta quietly says to Richmond.

Then she bends down and ruffles my fur. "Nipper, you go off with Richmond for a happy run."

Over the Ha-Ha

Whee!

Richmond and I spin once around the house checking on things.

   "Look out," Richmond calls to me as I take one great jump over the "ha-ha."

   Charlotta told me a ha-ha is like a ditch. There were sheep at Drayton Hall who "mowed the grass." Ha-has were dug to keep them from wandering into the garden and eating the flowers. The sheep are afraid to cross over the ha-ha, but I am not! Ha ha!! Let's go! But wait . . . Where is my ball?

   Richmond tosses it to me, waves, and takes off for the other side of the Big House. Wonder what in the world he is doing? Hmmm.

Inside the Big House

Lots to See

I think it's time for me to head inside for my first visit of the spring. I scamper up the steps of Drayton Hall and onto the portico which Charlotta has told me is a long word for porch, and then I prance inside. Emma and Sammy have opened the shutters in the Great Hall. Almost everyone enters this big room first when they come to visit.

I yip at the fox over the mantel that Charlotta calls a "cartouche," but that fox never makes a sound, no matter how much I yip. Still, dogs simply must yip at foxes. Charlotta says cartouche means "frame" in Italian.

I beeline for the stairs to the Upper Great Hall. Sometimes there are big parties here, and I often peek when no one is looking, so I can watch everyone having a good time. When I get up there today, I stare as I always do at those words HAC ITER AD ASTRA written near the bottom of the painting over the fireplace.

Charlotta told me those words mean, "This way to the stars." I like that! "This way to the stars."

Charlotta also explains that HAC ITER AD ASTRA is our Drayton family motto! She says families have a motto on their coat of arms to tell others what the family stands for, and they wore them on their armor a very long time ago. Charlotta knows everything!

The Growth Chart

Taller

Oh, I hear Charlotta calling me. "Nipper, it's time for you to be measured so we can see how much you have grown."

I run back through the Great Hall, "yip, yip" at the fox over the mantle, and scoot through the withdrawing room into the little dining room.

"Nipper?" Charlotta continues to call me. I spin around the corner. Then Charlotta measures me by having me stand up on my hind legs. She draws a line where my paws meet the door jamb and then writes down some numbers. She calls this a "Growth Chart," and it is only for the Drayton children and me, of course.

"Taller!" she exclaims. "You've grown just a bit since we measured you in April last year." I give a great "yip" and nip at the air. I even jump up as high as I can.

A Raised English Basement

Biscuits and a Nap

Whew . . . goodness, this last jump has made me very hungry! I snap up my ball and dart down the back steps into the Raised English Basement that is our kitchen. Charlotta heads to her bedroom, the small room upstairs where she will rest. She loves to sleep in that room because it has a window that lets cool air in at night, keeping things from being so hot.

"See there, Nipper, you must be hungry," I hear Emma say, and then she gives me my three o'clock dinner, including a few gravy biscuits left over from Charlotta's dinner.

By now, I am ready for my nap. So I settle down on my kitchen bed in the coolest corner of the basement near the ice box.

The Afternoon

Let's Play

When I wake from my nap, I jump up and down for Emma and Sammy.

"You headed out so soon?" Sammy asks.

I "yip," scoop up my ball, and then bolt upstairs to check on Charlotta, who is reading in the big room next to her bedroom.

"Good nap, Nipper, dear? Off now for your afternoon run around. Be careful and watch out for alligators." She has told me there have always been alligators in the river, and they love to swim around and eat fish and sometimes eat even bigger things. I think maybe she was talking about me! Yikes. Maybe it is time for a growl. Well, sometimes Charlotta worries too much.

"Yip! Yip!"

As I wander through the Great Hall, my ball gets ahead of me. Here I come.

Down to the River

Watch Out

Richmond comes running up the drive, and we take off towards the Ashley River with its dark water that flows all the way to Charleston. When I look into the water, I see my reflection and give a startled "yip!" I *always* think it is another dog who looks just like me and even has a ball that looks like mine!

While I am prowling along the water's edge, a duck suddenly appears along the riverbank and then disappears into the marsh. "Yip! yip!" Dogs must yip at ducks. Don't you agree?

I keep a look out for alligators, but *I* don't see one. Do you? I give a little growl just in case one is heading our way. They have a head that looks like a big old bumpy stone. Uh oh . . . There goes my ball heading right into the river. Here I go . . . whoops!

Suddenly Richmond grabs me and calls, "Don't you see that alligator?"

"Nipper! A little fella like you has to be careful. You'd make a nice supper for a big old alligator like that," gasps Richmond. Then suddenly I can see two eyes peering at me from the water. "Gr-r-r-r," I growl!

We shoot back towards Charlotta and the big house. When we find her, I hide behind her skirt.

"It was that alligator, Miss Drayton," Richmond bravely reports." But we made it." "Richmond, you saved Nipper's life. How very grateful I am. And now for you, Nipper, next time you must be on the lookout in case Richmond is not with you." I peek around. Charlotta reaches down and gives me a hug. Just what I needed.

But . . . Oh no! My ball! Gone! Then Richmond pulls my ball from his pocket and says, "Here you go, little fellow."

"Yip! Yip!" Nip! Phew! That was another close call.

Richmond pats me. "I'll see you later, puppy dog," and he heads off. He *is* my friend.

"Thank you again, Richmond," Charlotta calls and waves good bye.

Charlotta in the Garden

Painting and Taking Tea

That was exhausting. I really need a nap so I settle down next to Charlotta. She is sitting near the flower bed, painting in watercolors the beautiful azaleas and other spring flowers in blossom at Drayton Hall. When I wake up, I am feeling better. I sniff a few late blooming daffodils and take a nip at a leaf or two, careful not to let the bumble bee sting my nose!

Soon Emma brings Charlotta her tea, just like she does every afternoon at the same time between my afternoon nap and my last run around.

"Thank you, Emma," says Charlotta and smiles. They are good friends too . . . just like Richmond and me! "Yip."

I start to head off again for the river to look for ducks when Charlotta calls, "Nipper, remember your ball and do watch out for that alligator."

Hide-and-Seek

A Slip of a Puppy, a Slip of a Boy

I decide to look for my friend Richmond, who just saved my life, before I head to the river. I run a long way up the dirt road towards his house. When I first get there, Richmond is nowhere in sight, so I head over to the old graveyard and play a little game of hide-and-seek among the markers.

Then Richmond calls out, "Well, now, I think I spy the Business Man and his little red ball." I believe Richmond loves Drayton Hall as much as Charlotta and I do. And . . . he is awfully nice. He says I am just a "slip of a puppy dog!" Well, I think he's just a "slip of a boy" because he is not very tall or very old.

One of Richmond's favorite things to do is dig holes and put plants in them. He tells me he just planted a camellia, which he explains is a bush that often has red flowers. It is on the river side of the Big House. Another one of his favorite things to do is to throw my ball to me, of course. I run around him a few times for fun, and he tries to catch me. Nope. I am off! Yip! Richmond runs after me, and we head to the Ashley River to see it once more before the sun goes down. I want one last chance at any ducks we might find.

Day's End

The Last Run Around

As we get close to the river, I begin to wonder if that old alligator might be still there. Richmond stays close by as I crouch down very low and crawl to the river bank. That way if that old alligator *is* there, he won't see me. I continue rambling around, sniffing but not yipping or growling, just keeping an eye out for trouble. Richmond follows me. That's a good idea. As we walk the shores of the Ashley River, it moves along lazily.

Well, looks like there are *no* alligators. That's very good. Still I wish there were a few ducks so I could yip at them, but nope, not a one. The sun is starting to fade in the sky, and all is quiet so it must be getting late. Time to head home.

I scurry back to the big house, sniffing and nipping along the way, Richmond running beside me. When we get there, Richmond gives me a big hug before

he heads out for home. I know my friend Richmond and I will play again tomorrow and a lot of tomorrows. I "yip" one more good-bye.

Charlotta sees me and waves as she goes inside. It has been a very busy day! I find my way to the Raised English Basement and eat my supper of scraps and rice Emma has left for me in my bowl. Scrumptious! She and Sammy give me one last pat on the head.

"Good night, little fella," Sammy says, and then Emma leans down, hugs me, and smiles. "See you tomorrow." I turn some circles for them and try one last jump before I head up the back steps, but I am tired from my adventures so my jump isn't my best.

Hac Iter Ad Astra

This Way to the Stars

Then I stroll upstairs and "yip" good night to my old friend the fox, who still says nothing. Emma and Sammy have closed the shutters. I pick up my ball and make my way to Charlotta's bedroom. She is sitting in her chair reading, the oil lamp glows softly. She gives me a nice scratch behind my ears. I yawn and stretch, and then I peek out of the window. I wonder if Richmond is getting ready to go to sleep? Three circles around my upstairs bed, and I nestle in with my ball.

"Good-night, Nipper dear," Charlotta murmurs in a whisper.

"Yip!" . . . Nip . . . I sigh sleepily.

HAC ITER AD ASTRA

Postscript

Drayton Hall, located along the banks of the Ashley River outside Charleston, South Carolina, was established as a plantation in 1738, and built in the grand Palladian style by John Drayton. It belonged to the Drayton family until 1974, when it was purchased by the National Trust for Historic Preservation and the state of South Carolina with leadership and financial support from Historic Charleston Foundation and individual donors.

Charlotta Drayton Drayton (1884–1969), lovingly called "Aunt Charley" by her nieces and nephews, was the third child and youngest daughter of the four children of Eliza Merritt Gant and Charles Henry Drayton and was the last member of the Drayton family to spend any significant time at Drayton Hall. Charlotta was shy, a lover of travel, and a great reader. She took afternoon tea almost every day, and she painted with watercolors. Charlotta is buried in the Drayton family plot in Flat Rock, North Carolina, where her family had a summer home.

Over the years Charlotta Drayton expressed her desire that Drayton Hall stay the same as it was when she was there. Her family honored her wish in 1974 by transferring the property to the National Trust for Historic Preservation with an understanding that the Trust would not alter Drayton Hall. Since then, the Drayton family has donated and sold beautiful examples of their family pieces to Drayton Hall. Among them are a rare desk and bookcase (c.1745), china and silver as well as Drayton family diaries and journals, and also an extraordinary collection of 21 original watercolors of birds, painted by the Father of British Ornithology, George Edwards (1694–1773). Originally purchased in 1733 by eighteen-year-old John Drayton, the watercolors were rediscovered in Charlotta Drayton's attic at 25 East Battery in 1969. They are now the property of Drayton Hall, thanks to Charles Henry Drayton III and his family, Cindy and Ben Lenhardt, and many other donors to the Lenhardt Collection of George Edwards watercolors. The watercolors are exhibited on special occasions.

Nipper (1914–1929) was a black English Bull terrier and was said to "have the run of Drayton

Hall." Charlotta measured Nipper on April 8, 1915, and marked his progress on the Growth Chart on the door jamb in the room just off the withdrawing room (often referred to as the library). She would have him stand on his hind legs with his paws against the door jamb so he could be "taller." Nipper died February 5, 1929, and is buried at Drayton Hall down near the banks of the Ashley River. You can visit Nipper's grave marker when you come to Drayton Hall.

Richmond Herschel Bowens (1908–1998)
was born at Drayton Hall. His grandfather was a slave at Drayton Hall, and, according to his family's oral history, his ancestors came over as slaves from Barbados with the Draytons in the late seventeenth century. Along with Charles and Frank Drayton, Richmond represented the seventh generation in their respective family lines. Richmond is about seven years old when this story takes place. He lived in a house not far from the gatekeeper's cottage until he was fourteen and then moved to the nineteenth-century building that is now used as the museum shop. The camellia he was planting that day is still there along the River Walk. After being away for some years beginning in 1940, Richmond returned to work at Drayton Hall in 1974, and remained there until his death in 1998. Richmond worked as gatekeeper for a long time and when he retired, he continued to welcome visitors, often recalling family stories for them. On the back endpaper of this book is a rendition of Richmond Bowens' "Memory Map" of Drayton

Hall. He began helping archeologists find specific locations of house sites and other buildings on the property, and from that archeologists were able to locate many properties at Drayton Hall, including the location of Bowens' childhood home mentioned in this story. Richmond is buried at Drayton Hall in the African American Cemetery called the "Sacred Place" along with countless ancestors. He nicknamed Nipper the "Business Man."

Mary Emma Cook (b.1880) and **Samuel Middleton Cook**, according to U.S. Census records, lived with Charlotta's family at 25 East Battery in 1910. The census describes them as Samuel Middleton Cook, age 42, a coachman, and Mary E., his wife, age 30, the cook. The 1940 U.S. Census lists Charlotta as 55, and with her is widowed Emma Cook, a servant, aged 60. Samuel Middleton Cook was the son of David and Jane Cook, who had worked for the Draytons in 1880. Since Sammy's father had died at 25 East Battery, that address had become his home, not just a place of work.

Timeline

1679 Thomas Drayton sails from Barbados for the Carolinas. Richmond Bowens' ancestors may have arrived with him.

1715 John Drayton is born at Magnolia Plantation, next door to the property where he would eventually build Drayton Hall.

1733 John Drayton receives the collection of the 48 watercolors of birds painted by British ornithologist and artist George Edwards.

1738 John Drayton purchases the original 350 acre plantation property along the Ashley River, twelve miles from the city of Charleston. Over time he increased it to 650 acres. He is 23 years old.

1741 After his first wife dies, John Drayton marries Charlotta Bull. John and Charlotta have two sons, William Henry and Charles.

1747 John Drayton has a garden house built near the dock on the banks of the Ashley River. It is one of the first garden houses in the American South and remains an archeological site.

1780 British troops advance to Drayton Hall on March 23, 1780, after a skirmish at Church Creek. Later that year, the house becomes the headquarters of British General Charles Cornwallis. Two years later, General Anthony Wayne of the Continental Army establishes Drayton Hall as his headquarters while the British still occupy Charleston.

1855 Caesar Bowens (ancestor of Richmond Bowens), age fourteen, is among the people of African descent owned by Dr. John Drayton. After emancipation, Caesar stays at Drayton Hall, serving as caretaker.

1861 One of Drayton Hall's greatest mysteries is how it escaped the fate of other plantation homes along the Ashley River—almost all of which were burned. The most popular story is that Dr. John Drayton, great grandson of the founder of Drayton Hall, posted yellow flags at the entrances to the property indicating that it was being used as a smallpox hospital. Thus, the Union soldiers were afraid to go near Drayton Hall.

1865 Freedom comes to the slaves at Drayton Hall. Caesar Bowens and his brother John and sister Catherine remain at Drayton Hall and "take care of the place."

1886 Charlotta Drayton Drayton is born at 25 East Battery.

1908 Richmond Bowens, the grandson of Caesar Bowens and the son of Richmond and Anna Bowens, is born at Drayton Hall.

1969 Miss Charlotta, a member of the sixth generation of Draytons, dies. She leaves her share of Drayton Hall to her two nephews, Charles and Frank Drayton, each of whom already own a share inherited from their father. It is Charlotta's wish that "the property be preserved for further generations." Later that year, the George Edwards watercolors are rediscovered in her attic at 25 East Battery in Charleston.

1974 After thoughtful consideration, and rejecting an offer to turn it into a golf course and club house, Charles and Frank Drayton decide to sell the house and 125 acres to the National Trust for Historic Preservation and the remaining acreage to the state of South Carolina. Historic Charleston Foundation spearheads the campaign to raise funds for the purchase of Drayton Hall.

1998 Richmond Bowens, age ninety, dies. He is buried along with his family members and ancestors in the "Sacred Place," an African American Cemetery at Drayton Hall.

2006 Architectural historians from Colonial Williamsburg Foundation and other historical scholars or "history detectives" look for clues about how the house was built. Those clues are changing the understanding of Drayton Hall—from the shape of the original roof to the arrangement of ditches, drains, paths, and fields on the grounds.

2013 Drayton Hall turns 275 years old.

2015 Nipper's measurement on the Growth Chart celebrates its 100th anniversary!

Glossary

These are real things you can see at Drayton Hall today.

Cartouche — An Italian word for an ornate or ornamental frame. John Drayton was greatly influenced by works of the sixteenth-century Italian architect Andrea Palladio.

Coat of Arms — A coat of arms is an heraldic design used to cover and to identify the wearer. The design is a symbol unique to an individual person and to his family.

Growth Chart — On a door frame in a small first-floor room believed to have been the library and later called the little dining room, there is a growth chart of the Drayton children, dating from the mid-1890s, with their heights at various ages marked in pencil. The last family member to use the house, Charlotta Drayton, had no children. She measured the height of her dog, Nipper, on the opposite side of the door from the children.

Great Hall — The great hall served as a primary entertaining and welcoming space. Over the mantel you can still see the cartouche with the fox head, which might easily be mistaken for a boar or another animal. Nipper thought it looked a fox!

Hac Iter Ad Astra — The Drayton family Latin motto, "HAC ITER AD ASTRA," translates to "This way to the stars."

Ha-Ha — A Ha-ha is trench you cannot see from the garden. It is a physical barrier usually to keep out livestock on an expansive property such as Drayton Hall. You can see several Ha-has today at Drayton Hall. Be careful if you try to jump over one of them like Nipper did!

Large Bedchamber — This bedchamber is directly above the large yellow room. In the twentieth century, when Charlotta Drayton spent weeks at a time at Drayton Hall with no built-in electricity, she used one of these smaller rooms next to the large bedchamber as her bedroom. She could open the window in that room and therefore stay cooler on those warm spring days and nights.

Palladian—A style in architecture based on the work of Andrea Palladio, a sixteenth-century architect. When John Drayton built Drayton Hall built, he followed many of the rules set forth in Palladio's *The Four Books of Architecture* and copied designs from it.

Portico—A portico is an Italian word that means porch. Andrea Palladio was a pioneer in using porticos, a covered entry porch supported by columns.

Raised English Basement—The raised basement, a common feature in many of Palladio's designs, was a working space with storage and work areas. Today, there is a small room in the basement known as "Miss Charlotta's Kitchen." Her only "modern" additions to this space were a wood-burning stove and later, a Coleman stove, and an icebox that was later replaced by a refrigerator. This is the room where Nipper ate his meals and often took his naps.

Upper Great Hall—The ceilings in the Upper Great Hall are two feet higher than those on the first floor. The Upper Great Hall was the most important and elegant of the public spaces at Drayton Hall and the location of parties, dances, and musical entertainments.

Acknowledgments

My heartfelt thanks to:

My best friend, Anne Drayton Nelson, whose loving and helpful encouragement and supply of invaluable Drayton family history, kept me going until this project was completed.

Charles Henry Drayton III, Anne Drayton Nelson's father, who read this manuscript in its early days, and said, "I like it and so would Aunt Charley. You have my blessing."

Catherine Braxton and the Bowens family for their interest and support of this story.

George McDaniel, executive director of Drayton Hall, for his enthusiastic help in ensuring the historical accuracy of this story and for supplying me with factual information I needed.

Two of my favorite people: Dr. Nan Morrison, English teacher and retired chairman of the English Department of the College of Charleston, who read an early draft of "Nipper," and Nella Barkley, Co-founder and President of Chrystal-Barkley Corporation, who knew of my "Nipper" project, both of whom encouraged me to "Keep writing."

Michelle Gillett, my editor and Stockbridge, Massachusetts muse, without whose wise but gentle advice and suggestions, *Nipper of Drayton Hall* would never have gone to press.

Gerry McElroy whose charming and beautiful watercolor illustrations made Nipper and his family come alive.

Jonathan Haupt and Kim Shealy Jeffcoat at USC Press, whose vision for and belief in Nipper's story gave it the second chance it needed.

My children and grandchildren, in particular, my oldest grandson Holt who never failed to ask, "Nana, how's Nipper?"

My husband Tony who has believed in me from the beginning.

In memory of my parents, Monte and Douglas Parsons.

Royalties from the proceeds of this book go to fund the Interpretive Center at Drayton Hall.

And finally, I encourage you to visit this splendid place called Drayton Hall and to visit it often. Each season offers its own magic, each day lends itself to new discoveries. Long ago Nipper, Charlotta, Emma, Sammy, and Richmond along with many members of their families and their friends loved Drayton Hall. Today the Drayton and Bowens family members and their friends along with hundreds of visitors still love Drayton Hall. So will you. Under the watchful eyes of the Drayton Hall Preservation Trust and the National Trust for Historic Preservation, the main house of Drayton Hall remains much the same as it was in those days when Nipper used to run the grounds and scoot through the house with his favorite red ball, yipping and nipping in the air and occasionally growling. See you there.

Drayton Hall is open 360 days a year.

For more information visit www.draytonhall.org

40

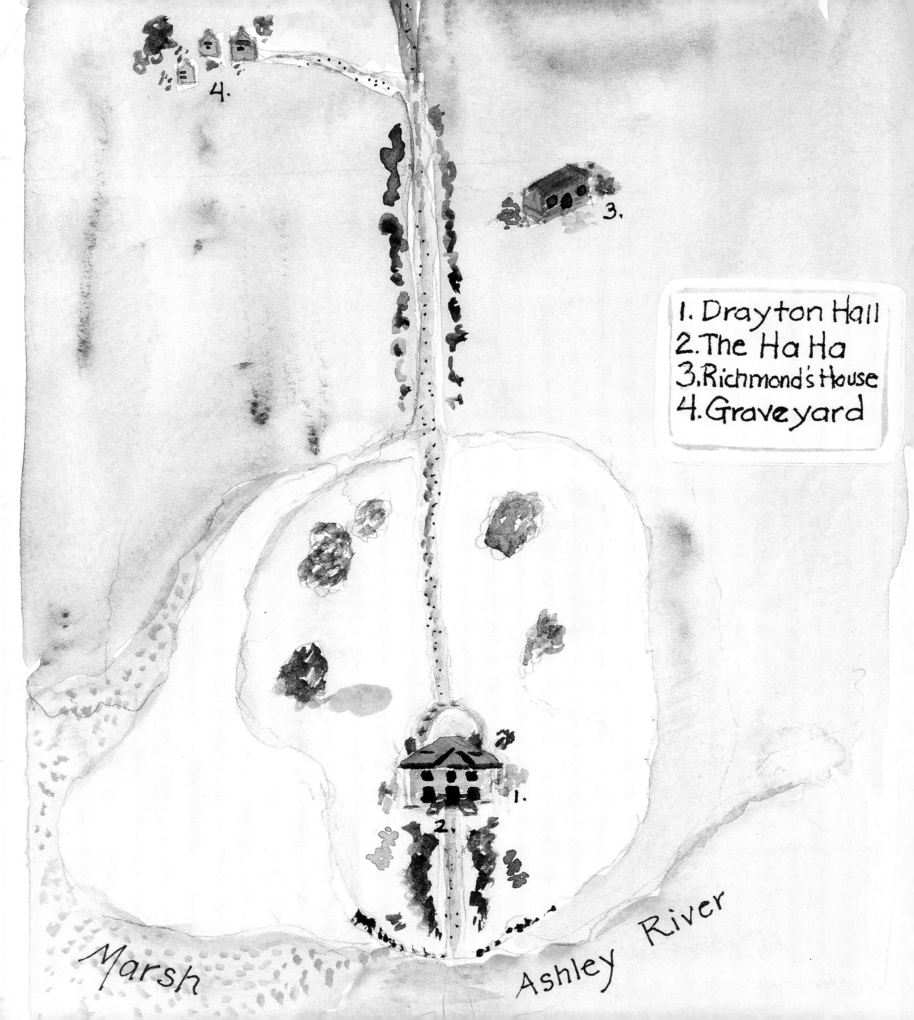

1. Drayton Hall
2. The Ha Ha
3. Richmond's House
4. Graveyard

Marsh

Ashley River